Coyote Volcano

A Shasta Tale

adapted by Michael Sandler
illustrated by Kathleen McCord

Harcourt

SCHOOL PUBLISHERS

Copyright © by Harcourt, Inc.

All rights reserved. No part of this publication may be reproduced or transmitted in any form or by any means, electronic or mechanical, including photocopy, recording, or any information storage and retrieval system, without permission in writing from the publisher.

Requests for permission to make copies of any part of the work should be addressed to School Permissions and Copyrights, Harcourt, Inc., 6277 Sea Harbor Drive, Orlando, Florida 32887–6777. Fax: 407-345-2418.

HARCOURT and the Harcourt Logo are trademarks of Harcourt, Inc., registered in the United States of America and/or other jurisdictions.

Printed in China

ISBN 10: 0-15-350552-4
ISBN 13: 978-0-15-350552-2

Ordering Options
ISBN 10: 0-15-350335-1 (Grade 5 Below-Level Collection)
ISBN 13: 978-0-15-350335-1 (Grade 5 Below-Level Collection)
ISBN 10: 0-15-357551-4 (package of 5)
ISBN 13: 978-0-15-357551-8 (package of 5)

If you have received these materials as examination copies free of charge, Harcourt School Publishers retains title to the materials and they may not be resold. Resale of examination copies is strictly prohibited and is illegal.

Possession of this publication in print format does not entitle users to convert this publication, or any portion of it, into electronic format.

5 6 7 8 9 10   468   12 11 10 09

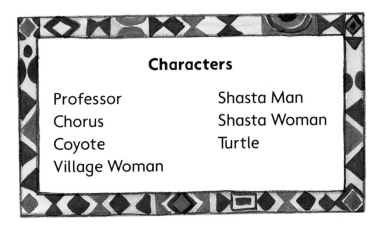

Characters

Professor
Chorus
Coyote
Village Woman

Shasta Man
Shasta Woman
Turtle

Professor: Class, today I will tell you about Coyote. He is a character in many Native American folktales. He had a reputation as a trickster. He had special powers. He could even change himself into a human. Today's story is about Coyote and California's Mount Shasta. Mount Shasta is a volcano. The tale tells why the volcano first erupted.

Chorus: Please get on with the story, Professor! We want to hear it!

3

Professor: For a time, Coyote lived in a village with people. Soon he grew tired of always eating the same food in the village. It was monotonous. He worried that he would wither away on such food.

Coyote: Do you know what I am yearning for? I want some fresh fish. I want to eat salmon.

Village Woman: Go to the Shasta village, Coyote. Their land is not parched and dry like ours. They dwell near rivers, lakes, and streams. The village residents build dams to trap fish. The Shasta always have salmon to eat.

Coyote: I will do just that. I am so hungry for salmon.

Professor: Coyote set out on his trip. The Shasta village was far away. He walked and walked for miles. Finally, he arrived.

Shasta Man: Welcome, Coyote. We seldom see you around here. What brings you around?

Coyote: I come for salmon, my friend. Do you think I could have some?

Shasta Woman: Of course, we have plenty! Our water is teeming with fish.

Professor: The Shasta man loaded one fish after another into a cloth sack. He put it onto Coyote's back. The bag was quite heavy. The Shasta man was very generous. Then Coyote began the long walk back to his village. He started out quickly, but he couldn't sustain the fast pace.

Coyote: My, this salmon is heavy. Carrying it is tiring. I think I will rest for a while.

Professor: Coyote lay down. While he slept, a swarm of rowdy bees saw Coyote's sack full of fish. They flew inside and ate it up. Nothing was left but bones.

Chorus: Professor, bees don't eat fish!

Professor: Coyotes don't talk either. This is just a story. Please let me continue. After a time, Coyote woke up.

Coyote: Ah, I feel so much better. I'll have a bite of salmon and keep walking. Hey, where's my salmon?

Professor: Coyote recoiled when he saw the bones. He was angry and began to bellow. He was also very confused. He looked in the dirt for tracks. There weren't any. Who had eaten his salmon? He decided to return to the Shasta village to get some more. Upon his arrival, he recounted the sorrowful tale.

Shasta Man: That is very strange!

Shasta Woman: I wonder who took your fish.

Shasta Man: It doesn't matter. Our water is brimming with salmon. We'll just get you some more.

Professor: The kind people of the Shasta village replenished Coyote's salmon supply. Then he headed off. Once again, he grew tired.

Coyote: I'm not making the same mistake twice. This time I won't go to sleep. I'll just lay here and rest.

Professor: Shortly thereafter, Coyote saw a swarm of bees. Coyote thought nothing of it. After all, he thought, bees don't eat fish. Coyote was in for a big surprise. This time the bees worked together and lifted up the whole sack. They flew off with it and vanished before Coyote could do a thing.

Coyote: It was the bees! I'm going to get those bees if it's the last thing I do!

Professor: The bees flew through the air. Coyote tried to follow. He couldn't keep up. Soon he came upon Turtle.

Turtle: What's your hurry, Coyote? There's no use in running fast.

Coyote: I'm looking for bees, Turtle. Have you seen them, by any chance?

Turtle: You mean the bees with the bag?

Coyote: That's right. They stole my fish.

Turtle: They headed that way—straight toward the top of Mount Shasta.

Professor: Coyote took off for the mountain. Climbing it was a difficult endeavor. When he finally got to the top, he found a hole. The bees had flown inside. He tried to elongate his body to squeeze into the hole, but he was much too big.

Coyote: I know what I'll do. I'll smoke out these salmon-stealing bees.

Professor: Coyote started a fire in the hole. Unfortunately, the smoke blew up, not into the hole. Coyote was hungry, angry, and exhausted. Running up the mountain had worn him out. He sat there throwing twigs on the useless fire. After a while, Turtle slowly crawled near.

Turtle: Coyote, you look awful. You should learn to slow down. Moving too fast will get you nowhere.

Coyote: I certainly haven't gotten anywhere. I can't even get to these pesky bees. I'm trying to smoke them out, but the smoke just rises out of the hole.

Turtle: Let me help.

Professor: Turtle sat down on the hole. His flat body covered it completely. Now the smoke was trapped. It built up inside the mountain.

Turtle: This shouldn't take too long.

Coyote: I hope not. I want my fish back. By the way, do you hear that noise?

Turtle: Noise?

Professor: A low rumble seemed to be coming out of the mountain. It grew louder and louder. Then, all of a sudden, there was a huge explosion. The top blew right off Mount Shasta. Smoke, steam, and rock poured into the air. Debris fell everywhere. The whole area was uninhabitable for weeks.

Chorus: What about Turtle and Coyote?

Professor: The two animals flew through the air, too. They landed miles away, right next to Coyote's village. They did not look very dignified covered with soot from the blast.

Village Woman: Coyote, you're back. How was your trip to the Shasta village?

Coyote: Not so good, I'm afraid.

Village Woman: You look a bit steamed.

Coyote: I am a bit steamed, and I never got my fish!

Turtle: Not so fast, Coyote. Have a look around.

Professor: Coyote looked around. All over the ground lay the salmon. It was steamed and smoked, perfectly cooked. Coyote and the villagers had a feast.

Chorus: That was excellent, Professor! We'd love to hear more about Coyote's escapades. Can we please have another story?

Professor: Maybe next week. I'll tell you how Coyote created the Columbia River.

Think Critically

1. What change in Mount Shasta does this myth explain?

2. Why does Coyote go to the Shasta village?

3. Do the Professor's students like the story? How do you know?

4. Why did Turtle sit over the hole where the fire was?

5. Do you like reading folktales? Why or why not?

 **Science**

Volcanoes Turtles don't cause volcanoes to explode, but what does? Look up volcanoes in an encyclopedia, reference book, or on the Internet. Find out what causes a volcanic eruption. Write a paragraph about the causes of volcanic eruptions. Draw a volcano diagram to accompany your paragraph.

 School-Home Connection Share this myth with a family member. What did they enjoy most about this Readers' Theater?